This Walker book belongs to:

Molly Mickelson

For Marie and Seamus – **M.M.**

For Sam and Grace – **E.C.C.**

First published 2008 by Walker Books Ltd, 87 Vauxhall Walk, London SE11 5HJ

This edition published 2010

2 4 6 8 10 9 7 5 3 1

Text © 2008 Michael Morpurgo Illustrations © 2008 Emma Chichester Clark

The right of Michael Morpurgo and Emma Chichester Clark to be identified
as author and illustrator respectively of this work has been asserted by them
in accordance with the Copyright, Designs and Patents Act 1988

This book has been typeset in Veljovik-Book

Printed in China

British Library Cataloguing in Publication Data: a catalogue record
for this book is available from the British Library

ISBN 978-1-4063-2620-8

www.walker.co.uk

WALKER BOOKS
AND SUBSIDIARIES
LONDON · BOSTON · SYDNEY · AUCKLAND

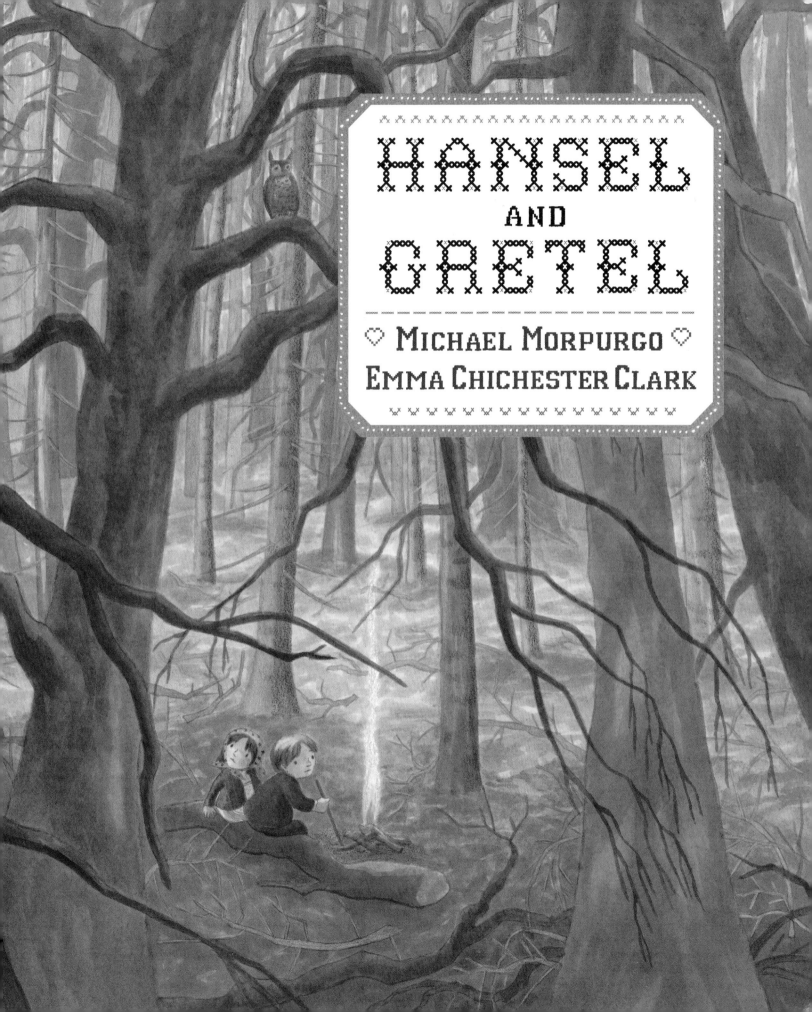

HANSEL
AND
GRETEL

♡ MICHAEL MORPURGO ♡
EMMA CHICHESTER CLARK

For Gabriel and Lisette,

every day seemed fine and sunny. They loved
one another deeply, and of course they hoped and
believed, as all young couples do, that they would live
happily ever after. Life seemed as perfect as it could be.
Everyone called them Gabriel the Good and Lisette the Lovely.
Very soon they were blessed with two wonderful children,
Hansel, and Gretel, his little sister. They all lived together in a
little thatched cottage on the edge of the forest. Here, they could
easily gather enough firewood to cook their food, and to keep
themselves warm through the winter. They could grow all the
vegetables they needed in the field of sweet earth. They had
eggs from the hens and milk from the cow that grazed on the
lush grass in the meadow. They gathered fruit and berries
and nuts. The river teemed with salmon and sea trout and
sometimes, for feast days, Gabriel would bring back a deer from
the forest. They were as happy as any family could ever hope to
be. Truly it seemed that God must be smiling down on them.

Then, one fine and sunny day, all that changed. Something
wicked came out of the forest, and she wasn't a wolf. She was
worse than the worst wolf ever could be. She was a witch,

a warty old witch, with gnarled skin like ancient treebark, a nose like a crabclaw, and her eyes glowed red, red as blood. Like all witches she was horribly cruel. Her greatest pleasure was to use her evil powers, all her wicked spells and enchantments, to cause as much mischief and suffering and grief as she possibly could. And this witch often didn't look like a witch at all. It was nothing for her to change herself into anything or anyone she wanted to be. But what she yearned for, as year by year she became older and uglier, as she ached more and more in her bones, as her eyesight grew dim and clouded with age, was to be young and beautiful. Above everything else, she longed to be loved.

When this gruesome old witch first happened to peep in through the cottage window and saw the family gathered inside, she came as a magpie, a cackling magpie, knocking on their windowpane. The children at once ran out and threw her some breadcrumbs, because they thought she might be hungry. And she *was* hungry too, but not for bread. She was hungry for something else entirely. Even as a magpie she could see only dimly. But that was enough. From the moment she first set her eyes on Gabriel, she loved him – loved him completely and utterly. And from the moment she first saw Lisette, she hated her just as completely, just as utterly. This woman had everything she so desperately wanted. She was radiantly beautiful, and she was so obviously loved and adored by everyone around her.

It's quite simple, thought the witch. I shall find a way to get rid of her. I shall take everything she has, her whole family. Then I shall have all I want. I shall be young and beautiful, even more beautiful than she is. I shall have Gabriel's love, and the love of his children too.

And what this wicked old witch wanted she always had, and never by fair means, always foul, the foulest means imaginable. Cruelty was her special speciality.

The next day Hansel and Gretel were down by the rushing river, by the stepping stones, helping their mother with the washing, as they often did. "You've worked hard enough for one morning, children," said Lisette. "You go off and play now, but not in the forest, mind. You know I don't like you playing there. There are wolves in the forest. Stay close to the house." So Hansel and Gretel kissed their dear mother goodbye, and ran off to play. High above them in the great oak tree, a magpie sat on a branch, quite unnoticed, and watched, and waited.

It was so easy. Once the children had gone, the magpie flew down and hopped silently towards Lisette who was still busy at her washing by the river's edge. It was nothing for the magpie to change herself, right there and then, into a beautiful young woman with green eyes and rose-red lips and chestnut-brown hair, nothing to cast a wicked spell on poor unsuspecting Lisette. "Be a tree," she whispered. "Be a tree, a weeping willow tree. Watch and weep. Watch and weep. All that you have, I will take. All that you are, I will be." And Lisette was turned, right there and then, into a weeping willow tree.

It was nothing for the witch, now this beautiful young woman, to throw herself into the river, to scream and shout, "Help me! Help me! She is drowning! She is drowning!" By the time Gabriel and the children came running, Lisette was gone, and instead they found a beautiful stranger, clambering exhausted and half drowned out of the water. "The river was too fast," she cried. "I

did all I could, but I couldn't save her. She was swept away."

They searched and they searched, but they could find no trace of Lisette, except the washing still left there on the river bank. They were all far too upset to notice that there was another weeping willow tree now growing near the very spot where Lisette had been washing their clothes. They did not hear it sighing for them in the breeze, crying for them in the wind. As for the beautiful stranger whom they all believed had nearly given her own life to try and save Lisette, Gabriel carried her home to their cottage and took her inside to look after her. She hardly had the strength to whisper her name. "Belladonna," she breathed. "I am Belladonna."

They gave her some dry clothes – Lisette's clothes seemed to fit her perfectly – and then Gabriel sat her down and gave her some piping hot soup. "Thank you," whispered Belladonna, and she looked deep into his eyes. Close to, she could see him a little better now, and he was even more handsome than she had thought. It seemed to good kind Gabriel that she was still far too weak to leave, so he laid her down by the fire to rest. And there she slept (or pretended to sleep). She slept for days and days. And whilst she slept Gabriel looked down at her and, despite his grief for Lisette, he was soon completely enchanted.

He thought she must be the bravest and, apart from Lisette of course, the most beautiful woman in the whole wide world.

Because of this, because of all she had done to try to save Lisette, and especially because she seemed so kind to the two children, it was only natural for Gabriel to ask her to stay on with them for a while. It was all turning out just as Belladonna had hoped and planned. And of course, the longer she stayed, the more bewitched Gabriel became. She's so lovely, he told himself. We could be happy together. Hansel and Gretel would have a new mother, and I would have a new wife.

When, a year or so later, he asked her to marry him, she was overjoyed. She threw her arms round his neck and kissed him. "I do love you so much," she said, "I'll make you the best wife. And I shall be the best mother to the children too. I love them so much – so much I could eat them."

On their wedding day, with everyone there, all their friends and family, with Hansel playing the flute and Gretel the fiddle, Gabriel and the beautiful Belladonna danced on the village green till the sun went down. There was hardly a whisper of wind that night, but still the weeping willow down by the river sighed and moaned all night long, so loud that neither Gabriel nor Belladonna could sleep.

"What's that strange noise?" Gabriel asked.

"I think it's that weeping willow tree," said Belladonna, and she was smiling to herself secretly in the darkness. "It sounds as if it's crying, don't you think? Almost as if it's in pain."

"You don't believe that trees have feelings, do you?" he said.

"Oh yes, they do," she replied. "Trees have feelings. And especially that one, I promise you."

Then after a little while, she went on: "Husband dearest, do you know what would make me truly happy, now that we are married, now that I am mistress in this house? I should like to make my first rule. I should like the children to call me 'Mother' from now on. Would you tell them? After all, I am their mother now, aren't I?"

"Isn't it a bit soon, dear?" Gabriel replied. "Maybe we should leave it a little while longer, until they have got to know you better, until they love you like a mother. Then they'll do it of their own accord, naturally."

"Don't you want to make me happy, husband dearest?"

said Belladonna. "Don't you love me as much as you love them?"

The last thing Gabriel wanted to do was to upset his new wife on their wedding night, so he agreed to tell Hansel and Gretel in the morning. But all night long as he lay there beside his new bride, listening to the willow tree sighing outside the window, he could think of nothing but poor, drowned Lisette, and how much he missed her.

In their bed downstairs, Hansel and Gretel could not sleep either. They were just too unhappy. "I know I should be pleased for Father," Gretel whispered. "I've tried and I've tried, but I just don't like Belladonna."

 "Neither do I," Hansel said. "There's something scary about her, about her eyes. Have you noticed how cold they are when she looks at you, cold as ice? It's like she's looking at you from far, far away, as if she can't see you properly. And when she smiles, she only smiles with her lips, not her heart. And her lips are as red as blood."

"I wish Mother was here," Gretel whispered, "I miss her so."

"Me too," said Hansel. And they hugged each other tight, and cried, silently so that no one could hear them. But Belladonna did hear them. She might not be able to see very well, and she still ached in her bones – whatever shape she took on, she could never seem to escape her old infirmities – but she had heard every word they'd said, because like all witches, she could hear and smell perfectly, just as well as the animals can. And what she had just heard made her angry, very angry indeed.

At breakfast the next day, as he had reluctantly agreed, Gabriel told the children that from now on they should always call Belladonna "Mother". "You can call me Mother or Mama, dearest children," said Belladonna, in her sweetest voice. "Whichever you like." But when Hansel and Gretel were silent, she knew very well that they liked neither. A little later, Belladonna followed them down to the river.

For some reason, the children always felt safe there, under the fronds of the branches of the weeping willow tree by the stepping stones. This was where they went when they wanted to be alone together. But they weren't alone, not that morning. Belladonna was there, hidden behind the bushes, and listening to every word.

"I won't do it," Hansel was saying. "I won't call her Mother, no matter what."

"And anyway, she's not our mother," Gretel cried. "I only have one mother, and she's dead."

Belladonna heard it all. She was seething with fury. She had done all she could to make the children love her, forced herself to be as kind and sweet to them as possible, and still they resented her, still they longed for Lisette. The time for kindness and sweetness was over. It was time to make the children suffer.

"Husband dearest, children dearest," she said at supper that evening, as sweet as sweet could be. "I think I'd like to make just one more little rule, if you don't mind. You know that all I want is for us to be happy together, don't you? Because of this, I think it would be best if no one ever spoke of Lisette again. After all, she's dead now and gone for ever, isn't she? Why don't we just forget her?"

But Hansel and Gretel could not forget her. They didn't want to forget her. Neither did Gabriel. With every day that passed, his doubts about Belladonna were growing. There was something about her that was beginning to alarm him. And, though they never said as much to their father (for fear of offending him), the children were feeling the same, only more so. They were beginning to hate Belladonna, and the more they hated her, the more they longed for their dear, dead mother, and the more they talked about her in secret under the fronds of the weeping willow tree. But whenever they talked about her, Belladonna overheard every word they said, and every word only enraged her more.

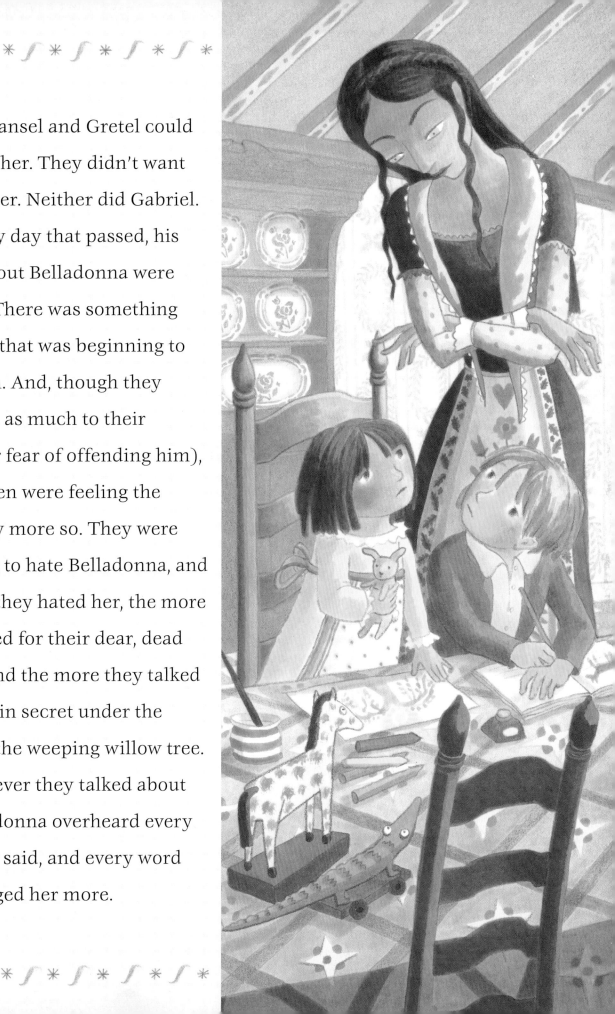

And there was something else that angered her just as much. Every time she saw Gabriel out playing with Hansel and Gretel, she could hear the joy in their laughter. She may not have been able to see them very well, but she could tell just how much he loved them. He seemed to want to spend more and more time with them, and less and less with her. There's only one thing for it, she thought. I'll have to get rid of the children too. With them dead and gone like their mother, then all reminders of Lisette will be gone forever, and then I can have Gabriel to myself.

But it wasn't enough for Belladonna simply to click her fingers and make them disappear in a puff of smoke, or turn them into snails or frogs or worms – she could have done that only too easily. It would have been nothing for her to do that. No, she wanted Gabriel to have to do the deed himself. Somehow she would persuade him to abandon his own children. That way it would be the proof she needed that he loved her more than he loved them. As for the children, she so disliked them by now, was so jealous of them, that she didn't mind how much they suffered – the more the merrier, as far as she was concerned – just so long as in the end she could have Gabriel to herself. It didn't take Belladonna very long to work out the best way, the cruellest way all this could be achieved. And the first step, she decided, was to put a curse on the countryside all around, on all the wild things, all the plants and creatures. She would create a famine. She'd done it before. She was good at creating famines, and what's more she enjoyed it too, because in a famine everyone suffered horribly.

The very next morning the birds stopped singing. The flowers began to die, and all the bees and butterflies with them. There were no fish anymore in the rivers and streams. All the vegetables and corn rotted in the ground. Soon there was nothing left for the animals to eat. First the cow had to be killed, then the hens. Every day Gabriel had to go deeper into the forest scavenging for berries and mushrooms and roots, but there were scarcely any left to find. There were no animals to hunt either, no deer, no wild boar, no rabbits. Only the wolves survived in the forest, and they were howling in their hunger, night and day.

It was the worst famine anyone had ever known. Everyone was surviving only on the few berries and roots they could still find. There was nothing else to be had.

By this time Hansel and Gretel were weak with hunger, crying out in their pain and misery, begging their father for food. Gabriel was in despair. There was nothing he could do. Belladonna knew this was her moment to act. "Husband dearest," she whispered to him one night, as they lay listening to the children weeping downstairs. "They are starving. We will all starve if we go on like this. I couldn't bear to see you die. And you don't want me to die, do you dearest?"

"Of course not," Gabriel replied. "But what more can I do?"

"I think I may know a way, husband dearest," said Belladonna, "that you and I could be eating twice what we are eating now."

"How?"

"It's very simple, dearest. If Hansel and Gretel were not here, then there would be more for us, wouldn't there? All you have to do is 'lose' them somehow, that's all."

"That's all!" cried Gabriel. "I can't. I couldn't do it."

"I'm not suggesting you kill them, nothing like that," Belladonna replied. "All you have to do is take them into the forest and leave them there."

"But they'll starve," Gabriel pleaded, "either that, or the wolves will eat them."

"Maybe," said Belladonna, "but either way we shall have two less mouths to feed. Don't you see, it's either them, or me, dearest husband."

"But they're my children!" Gabriel cried. "I'd be abandoning my own children!"

At this Belladonna turned her back on him and wept. "I see you don't love me enough," she wailed, "You might as well go downstairs right away and make coffins for all four of us, and we can just climb in and die. Would that make you feel any happier? Would it?"

"No, of course not, but..."

"No buts, dearest," said Belladonna firmly. "Do it in the morning. The sooner, the better. Trust me. It's the only way. Just take them to the forest and get it over with. Promise me you will."

"If I must," Gabriel replied with a heavy heart, "if it is the only way." But even as he was speaking, Gabriel could not believe what he was saying. Neither could he believe that Belladonna, whom he had once loved so much, was telling him he should abandon his own children. The truth was that he loved Hansel and Gretel more than life itself. No, he could not do it, he would not do it.

He lay there, struggling with his conscience, and struggling to find some way he could save them without Belladonna finding out. In the early hours, leaving her fast asleep, he got up and went to sit under the weeping willow tree. Just like the children, he'd taken to going there whenever he wanted to think things through. It was the place he loved best, the place he felt closest to his beloved Lisette.

He sat there by the river, his head in his hands. "What shall I do, Lisette?" he cried. "I have been so stupid. I know I should never have married her. What can I do? How can I save the children?" And all at once the tree seemed to shiver above him and whisper to him, its fronds caressing his head. As Gabriel opened his eyes the moon came out from behind the clouds, and at that same moment he saw the river stones glowing white beneath the water. He knew at once what had to be done.

He stole silently back to the cottage, gathered some bread for the children, woke them and told them to get dressed. "But it's still dark. Where are we going so early, Father?" Gretel asked him.

"To the forest," he replied. "No noise now. I don't want to wake Belladonna." They left without a sound and made for the stepping stones over the river. As soon as they had crossed, and Gabriel thought they were far enough away from the cottage not to be heard, he stopped and told them everything: how Belladonna wanted him to abandon them in the forest because there wasn't enough food to feed all four of them. "But I can't do it, children," he told them, "because I love you far too much. Belladonna may well be right. We may all die in this dreadful famine, but if we do, I've made up my mind we'll do it together. So follow me, children, and do just what I do."

Silently, silently, Hansel and Gretel followed their father along the river bank to where the river stones were white and bright in the moonlight. And when he began to pick them up and stuff them in his pockets, they did the same. They picked up all they could, until their pockets were full.

"What are we doing this for, Father?" Hansel asked.

"You'll soon see," Gabriel said. Then off they went into the forest, deeper and deeper, and as they went Gabriel told them to drop their stones behind them one by one, every now and then. "All you have to do, children, is follow these little white stones," he explained, "and you'll easily be able to find your way back home.

And when you do come home, we must all pretend that when I took you into the forest you just wandered off and got yourselves lost. Remember, children, this must be our secret. Not a word to Belladonna. Never. You promise?"

"We promise," said Hansel and Gretel.

All morning long they walked on into the silent forest, and all the way they left a trail of little white stones behind them. No birds sang, no stag bellowed. It was a dead place, a dark place. At about noontime they came into a clearing. "This is far enough, I think," said Gabriel. "I'll light a fire to keep you warm. It'll keep away the wolves too. They hate fire. They won't come near you, don't worry. When night falls, just wait for the moon to rise, and you'll be able to follow the little white stones all the way home. But you must wait for the moon to rise, children, or you won't be able to see the stones, and you'll get lost." So he lit the fire, and gave them the little bread he had, enough to keep their strength up. He hugged them tight, and told them to be sure to keep the fire burning brightly. Then, after praying with them for their safe return, he left them and went on his way back home.

When he got there, Belladonna was waiting for him at the door. "Well, have you done as I said, dearest husband?" she asked him.

"You did leave them deep in the forest, didn't you, so deep they can never find their way out?"

Gabriel could only nod in reply, hanging his head so she could not see the truth in his eyes. "Don't look so sad, husband dearest," said Belladonna, putting her arms around him. "They are gone now. Forget them. Now we will have enough food to see us through this famine. Now we can be happy, just the two of us. And one day we can have children of our own. Wouldn't that be wonderful, dearest?" But even as she spoke Gabriel could feel the last of his love for her draining away. When he looked up at her now, he discovered she was not beautiful to him anymore.

Meanwhile, deep in the forest, Hansel and Gretel sat by their fire, waiting for night to come and sharing their last crumbs of bread. They heard the first howling of the wolves in the forest, and both of them shivered with fear. "Oh please Hansel, let's go, let's go now," cried Gretel. "I'm so frightened. I hate it here!"

"I hate it here too," Hansel replied, trying his very best not to sound scared. "Don't worry, the wolves won't come near the fire. That's what Father told us, remember? And he said we have to wait for the moon to rise, didn't he, so we can see the little white stones in the moonlight. Otherwise we'll just get lost in the forest, and then we'll never find our way home at all."

So hand in hand they stayed by the fire till the moon rose above the trees and they could see at last the trail of little white stones leading away into the forest. Now they could go. So Hansel and Gretel left the fire, and ran off, the white stones guiding them homewards. But where they went the wolves soon followed. The children could hear them howling all around them. They could see their eyes glinting in the moonlight.

"They're coming closer," cried Gretel. "They're going to kill us and eat us up!"

"No they won't," said Hansel, still trying to be as brave as he could. "They're not hungry. Forget them. Just keep looking for the next stone. We'll soon be home now."

But after one little white stone there was always another and another

and another, and they could see the wolves' eyes all around them. They could hear them padding and panting out there in the darkness. They could imagine them licking their lips.

"Oh, how much further can it be?" cried Gretel. "How much further?"

"Not far now," said Hansel. But in fact, he had no idea at all how far they had to go. Worse still, the wolves had begun to howl again, and he knew only too well what they must be telling each other: Time to eat, time to kill. Time to eat, time to kill.

Then Hansel had a sudden idea. "Let's sing, Gretel," he said. "They're howling. Well, we can howl too, can't we? It'll show them we're not afraid. Sing, Gretel, sing!" And so they sang. They sang every song they knew, as loudly as they could, over and over again till their throats were raw, so loudly they couldn't even hear the wolves howling around them any more.

Back in the cottage, Gabriel couldn't sleep. He was far too worried to sleep. He kept hearing the wolves howling out there in the forest. He got up and went to the window, longing to see Hansel and Gretel come running home. But they didn't come and they didn't come.

"What are you looking at, husband dearest?" Belladonna

asked him, getting out of bed and coming to the window.

Gabriel had to make something up very quickly. "I thought it was the white cat on the roof." He told her. "But it's not, it's the morning sun rising over the chimney." Then Gabriel heard something, and opened the window. Children! It was the sound of children singing loudly, very loudly indeed. And out of the forest came Hansel and Gretel, hand in hand.

"Well, would you believe it!" cried Gabriel. "It's the children! Isn't that amazing? They've found their way home, all on their own. How on earth did they manage that?" He ran downstairs at once and rushed outside. From the window Belladonna could only watch, her dark heart full of fury, as Gabriel threw his arms around the children, hugging them and kissing them. "I searched for you everywhere, children. I thought I had lost you for ever!"

And all this was said out loud, loud enough for Belladonna to hear every word. "Why did you go wandering off like that?" he went on. "Didn't I tell you to stay close by me in the forest?" He glanced up at Belladonna at the window, "Isn't it wonderful, Belladonna? They're safe! They've come home!"

"Wonderful," said Belladonna, smiling through clenched teeth, a smile that was as false as it was murderous and cruel. Next time, she thought, next time there'll be no mistake. One way or another I shall rid myself of those children once and for all.

The weeks passed, and it soon became clear to Belladonna

that neither Hansel nor Gretel would even bring themselves to look at her, let alone speak to her. Until now they might not have called her "Mother", but they had at least been polite. Now they just ignored her. When they were with their father they were always smiling and happy. Worse still, Gabriel was smiling and happy with them too, so much happier than he ever was with her. The more jealous she became, the more she got it into her head that perhaps Gabriel had quite deliberately not taken them far enough into the forest before he abandonded them, that somehow he had helped them find their way home again, helped them survive. After all, hadn't he been ecstatically happy to see them that morning when they came home safe and sound? Hadn't he hugged them and kissed them? Gabriel must have had a hand in it, she was sure of it. The next time she would make quite certain the children didn't come back. And the next time, she decided, would be very soon, as soon as possible.

One stormy night with thunder and lightning crashing round the cottage, with rain and wind lashing the windows, Gabriel woke up in bed to find Belladonna beside him hardly able to breathe. She lay there gasping, her cheeks sunken, her face as pale as parchment, her lips blue with hunger – it was nothing for her to make herself look like this. "I am dying of hunger, dearest husband," she whispered. "Every mouthful you feed to those children is killing me, can't you see? How can you do this to me? Didn't I leap into the river and risk my life to save Lisette? Haven't I always tried to be a good and kind mother to Hansel and Gretel? I beg you, take them to the forest again, and leave them. But this time go deeper into the forest, deeper still. If you let them stay here one more day, they will starve me to death."

Gabriel looked down at his poor starving wife. Even if he didn't love her any more, he knew he could not refuse her. But neither could he bring himself to abandon his children. "Do it now dearest," she breathed, clutching his hand. "Do it now, while I still have breath in my body. Tell me you'll do it. Promise me."

"I promise," said Gabriel. But even as he was getting out of bed, he knew exactly what he was going to do. I'll do just what I did before, he thought. It worked fine. Belladonna didn't find out then, and she won't find out now.

He woke the children up, wrapped them up as well as he could against the cold and the wind and the rain, gathered some bread for them to eat in the forest, just as he'd done before, and set off with them to collect the little white stones from the river. But as they ran across over the stepping stones, they could see that the river was high all around them, and rushing by under the trees. And to their horror they discovered that all the river stones were covered by swirling floodwater.

The three of them stood there sheltering under the weeping willow tree, wondering what could be done.

"Without the little white stones to guide us, we're never going to be able to find our way out of the forest," said Hansel.

"What shall we do, Father?" Gretel cried.

Above them the tree wafted its branches and whispered in the wind, the fronds caressing their heads. All at once Gabriel knew what he had to do. "We'll be all right, children," he said. "Follow me!" And they ran off into the forest. Behind them, if they had looked, they'd have seen the weeping willow tree waving frantically after them, trying to warn them. And they would also have seen a magpie flitting from tree to tree, silently. It was Belladonna, following close behind them, quite close enough to see them stop under a great oak tree, close enough to see Gabriel empty his pockets and give the bread to the children. She heard every word he said to them.

"We can do it with this bread, children," he told them, "just as we did with the little white stones. Every now and then we'll drop these pieces of bread behind us. The rain has stopped now, and the sky is clearing. As soon as the moon is out tomorrow night, you'll be able to follow them home, just like you did before." And off they went, deeper and deeper into the forest, leaving a trail of breadcrusts behind them, to mark their way home.

None of them noticed the magpie that was flitting through the darkness, silently, following them, silently. She saw them come out of the forest into the clearing, saw Gabriel light the fire, and Hansel and Gretel fetching the wood. "Now remember, children," Gabriel was telling them, "you must wait until the moon comes up. Then you just follow the bread trail home. And not a word to Belladonna. This is our secret. She must believe you got lost and found your own way home, like last time. Be brave, and I'll see you very soon. God bless you."

And with that he hugged them tight, said a parting prayer with them, and walked away into the forest, right under the very branch where the magpie was perched, watching everything with her beady black eye. Only once Gabriel was well out of sight did she fly to the ground. How very kind and thoughtful of them to leave me their bread, she thought to herself.

I think I feel a little peckish. I think I'll help myself. So, hopping all the way back to the cottage, she helped herself to every piece of bread they'd left behind, down to the very last crumb.

Of course, it was nothing for her to fly home ahead of Gabriel. By the time Gabriel got home himself, he found Belladonna lying in bed – still, apparently, barely able to speak. "You did take them deep into the forest this time, husband dearest, as deep as you could possibly go?" she asked him.

"If they find their way out this time," Gabriel replied, "it'll be a real miracle."

"Do you know, husband dearest," said Belladonna. "I'm feeling so much better already."

Gabriel was very tired after his long walk in the forest, but all the same, he sat up all night by the window, waiting for Hansel and Gretel to return. "What are you looking at, husband dearest?" said Belladonna, getting up from her sickbed to join him.

Again, Gabriel had to think very quickly. "I thought I saw a little white dove on the roof," he told her, "but it wasn't. It was just the rising moon sitting on the barn roof."

"Come back to bed and sleep, dearest," said Belladonna.

But Gabriel was far too worried about the children to think of sleeping. He went outside and sat on the river bank under the weeping willow tree, and prayed aloud that the children would find their way home safe and sound. As he prayed, the fronds caressed his hair, and the whole tree began to murmur gently to him. It was so soothing, so comforting that he soon fell fast asleep.

He couldn't know it, but deep in the forest the children were very far from safe and sound. They were still sitting by the fire, longing for the moon to shine more brightly, but already the wolves were beginning to howl horribly all around them.

Despite this, they did just as Gabriel had told them. They waited till the moon was up and then set off home. "All we have to do is follow the breadcrusts," said Hansel. "And we'll sing as we go, so we'll sound as brave as we did before. We howled as loudly as the wolves did last time, didn't we? And they didn't eat us, did they?"

So singing out loudly, and hand in hand, they left the fire and walked away into the forest, searching for the bread trail they'd left behind them the day before. They looked and they looked, but they couldn't find any bread anywhere, not a crumb, not a crust. They just couldn't understand it. Hansel tried his best to stay cheery, but it wasn't easy. "Don't worry, Gretel," he said. "We'll stay by the fire till morning. We'll keep ourselves warm, and the wolves won't come near us. We can find our way home in the morning, when it gets light. We'll be fine."

But when morning came, they weren't fine at all. Try as they did, with no bread trail to follow, they could not find their way out of the forest. They kept going round and round in circles, and then finding themselves back in the clearing by the fire. By now they were so hungry and thirsty and tired that they hadn't even got the strength to fetch the wood they needed to keep the fire going. All they could find to eat were one or two

shrivelled up berries, but every time they saw one, a magpie came down and ate it before they could even pick it, and then flew away cackling like a witch. As the sun went down again they sat shivering over the dying embers of their fire.

"Father will come looking for us, won't he?" said Gretel, faint with hunger now.

"Of course he will," Hansel told her, trying hard to believe it himself. "He wouldn't leave us out here to die. Let's sing, Gretel, sing out loud, so Father can hear us, and come for us. He won't be long."

They couldn't have known what had happened back at home, that their poor father was still sitting on the river bank under the weeping willow tree, that Belladonna had overheard him talking to Lisette, and praying out loud for Hansel and Gretel to come home safe and sound. She had been so enraged that she had at once cast

a wicked spell on him and turned him to stone. It was nothing for her to do that.

"Now I can be quite, quite sure," she said to herself, "that Gabriel will never be able to rescue them, that Hansel and Gretel will never ever come out of the forest alive. If he doesn't love me enough to do it for me, then to hell with him, I'll just have to get rid of them myself. It will be a pleasure. I shall enjoy that, I shall enjoy it very much indeed."

The next morning, after a long and sleepless night, the children tried to find their way home, tried once more to find something, find anything to eat. But all the while they were becoming weaker and weaker, too weak now even to sing. They could not go another step further. In the end they lay down in the hollow of an old elm tree, held hands, closed their eyes and waited for the wolves to come and eat them.

At first they both thought they must be dreaming. Above them on a branch was a magpie, but it was no ordinary magpie because it was speaking to them. "Little children," it was saying, "little children, I know somewhere, and it's not far off, where you can find all the food you could ever eat and all the water you could ever drink. Follow me, I'll show you." And with a cackling laugh the magpie flew off.

Hansel and Gretel helped one another to their feet and followed where it flew. Just the thought of all that food and drink gave them new strength. The bird had been right too, right about everything. It wasn't far. They soon came to a stream where the water was shining and clear. They knelt down and drank their fill. When they looked up, they saw a cottage in the distance with a farmyard all around. It looked just like home.

They ran as fast as they could towards the cottage. But as they came closer they realized it wasn't their home at all. It couldn't be, because this cottage wasn't made of stone and wood and thatch. Instead, amazingly, it was built of sugar-coated gingerbread! And the roof was made of pink icing sugar. The chimney was a stick of barley sugar! As for the window frames, they were marzipan, and the panes of glass were the purest sugar! The front door was made entirely of shortcake. "It's marzipan!" cried Hansel, tucking in without a thought. "My favourite!"

They were soon both so busy eating that they never noticed

the magpie fly down the chimney. But moments later they did hear the sound of a strange voice coming from inside the cottage.

"Nibbledeeday, nibbledeeday. Who's nibbling at my house today?" Suddenly the front door flew open, and out came a jolly looking old lady, with plump cheeks and little fatty fingers, bustling towards them, arms outstretched.

"Welcome, welcome, dear sweet children," she said. "You must have got lost in the forest. Oh, you're so sweet. I could eat you, I really could. But you look so thin. I prefer children to be fat, but I can arrange that. All you have to do is eat. Come along inside. I could make you pancakes with golden syrup. Would you like that?"

The children couldn't say a word, because they were so surprised, because they couldn't believe their luck and because their mouths were so full. But they could nod, and they did so, vigorously.

"I'll look after you," said the jolly old lady, leading them inside. "You'll be quite safe with me, safe as houses."

Once they were inside she sat them down at the kitchen table and fed them on pancakes and golden syrup until they couldn't eat another mouthful. After they had finished she took them into a room with two little beds all made up with white linen sheets. Never had beds looked so soft and inviting. "Sleep tight, little children," said the jolly old lady, tucking them in. "Sweet dreams."

"Are you sure this isn't a dream?" Gretel whispered when the little old lady had gone. "I mean, isn't it all just a little too perfect? Suddenly all the food we want, and a warm bed. Isn't she just a little too good to be true?"

"I don't care," Hansel replied, half asleep already. "If it is a dream, then it's the best dream in the world and I don't ever want to wake up. Go to sleep."

But Gretel couldn't sleep. "There's just something about her that worries me," she said, "something I recognize, I think. Her voice maybe. No, it's her eyes. They're cold, cold as ice. And she doesn't see very well, I can tell. I don't like her, and I don't trust her, Hansel. Hansel?"

But already Hansel was fast asleep. And very soon Gretel was asleep as well, far too tired to worry any more about the jolly old lady. When she dreamed that night, she was back home in her own bed, and her mother, the lovely Lisette, was tucking her in and singing her a lullaby, like she always used to at bed time. She was singing so sweetly, like a lark rising into the blue, but then Gretel realized it wasn't a lark anymore. It was a magpie, tapping at her window, cackling noisily and glaring at her with black beady eyes. Suddenly this magpie had turned into the beautiful Belladonna. She was smiling down at her, but her smile was false and her eyes were cold, and as she tucked her in she became the jolly old lady with the plump red cheeks and little fatty fingers.

That was when Gretel came out of her dream, opened her eyes and found a warty old hag peering into her face, her skin gnarled like ancient treebark, her nose like a crab claw, her eyes glowing red, red as blood. At that moment Gretel knew and understood everything, that the magpie and Belladonna and the jolly old lady were one and the same, that she was staring up into the face of a witch, a wicked, cruel witch. "Get up, you lazy bones," the witch croaked, grasping her with her skinny hand. Gretel cried out for Hansel, but he was not in his bed. "He can't help you now," cackled the warty old witch. "And you can't help him. But you can help me, and you will. Come and look. Come and look." And she dragged Gretel off outside to show her what she had done.

There in the corner of the farmyard she saw poor Hansel cowering at the back of a dark and dingy cage, like an animal. And outside the cage, guarding him, there was a snarling, slavering wolf with big sharp teeth.

"Now at last, I shall be rid of you both for ever," shrieked the witch. "It's Hansel's turn first. Do you know what I'm going to do with him? I'm going to fatten him up, put him in the oven and roast him. That's what I'm going to do. Then I'll gobble him up till there's nothing left but knuckles and toes." The wolf came grovelling up to her, and she patted his head with her knobbly fingers. "Wolfdog likes those himself, don't you my dear? Then Gretel, dear sweet Gretel, apple of your father's eye, I'm going to do the same to you."

She pinched her finger and squeezed her arm. "You're a bit too skinny, so I'll be eating Hansel first. But I must have him fatter, and you're going to make him fatter for me. I want him nice and plump. Cutlet of roast boy with gravy, and some nice crusty bread. Buttered parsnips and boiled beetroot to go with him, and lots of pepper and parsley. Delicious. Delightful. Delectable. Then I'll fatten you up and do the same for you, only with carrots and leeks. Girls always taste better with carrots and leeks." She bent down and glared deep into Gretel's eyes. "And don't you ever think of running away or I'll turn you into a rabbit, and let Wolfdog hunt you down and tear you to bits. He's very good at that, aren't you, Wolfdog, my dear? Oh, and by the by, sweet Gretel, don't even think of talking to Hansel, not even a whisper. Remember, I'm a witch, and I can hear a whisper a mile away."

So for weeks on end the witch made Gretel cook for her: buttered scones and battered sausages, pancakes and pies, cheesecake and chicken. At every meal Hansel had a huge pile of food to eat, and Gretel had to make sure he ate it. "Take it out to him, and mind you bring me back a clear platter," she was told. "Plump and podgy, that's how I want him." And Gretel did just as she said, or the wicked witch thought she did anyway, because she always brought the platter back empty.

But all the while, unbeknown to the warty old witch, Gretel had been working out a cunning way of fooling her. She knew perfectly well by now, of course, that this wicked witch could do almost anything she wanted. She could turn you into a rabbit or a toad, into anything or anyone she felt like. After all, hadn't she turned herself into a magpie, into Belladonna, into a jolly old lady?

Hadn't she made a cottage of gingerbread and marzipan? But Gretel had noticed that, just like Belladonna, her eyes were weak, that the old witch didn't seem to be able to see at all well. In fact, her eyes were so dim that there was only one way she could tell just how fat Hansel really was. Every evening the warty old witch would hobble out of the cottage and across the farmyard over to Hansel's cage. When she got there, she'd always say the same thing. "Stick out your finger, Hansel," she'd say. Then, to test how much fatter he'd got, she'd squeeze his finger tight. But every time she'd let out a screech of rage. "No fatter! No fatter!" she'd shriek. "What's the matter? What's the matter? More batter on his platter! More batter on his platter!" She couldn't understand it. Every evening Hansel's finger was just as bony as ever.

What she didn't know was that Gretel was giving Hansel only very little of each meal – just enough to keep him alive and well, but no more. The rest she gave to Wolfdog, who was only too pleased to lick the platter clean every time. What she couldn't see (and this was Gretel's most brilliant idea of all), was that it wasn't Hansel's finger she was squeezing at all, but an old chicken bone instead. So every time she squeezed it, she found Hansel's finger was just as skinny and bony as the evening before,

and she was furious. She would screech and shriek and stamp her foot. And every time, Gretel told her: "I'm sure he'll be fatter by tomorrow evening." But when tomorrow evening came Hansel would stick out his chicken bone finger again, and of course to the wicked old witch, it always felt just as skinny as before. "I'm sure he'll be fatter by tomorrow," Gretel would tell her yet again. But he never was. The old witch became furiouser and furiouser. At this rate Hansel would never be fat enough to eat – which was of course precisely what Gretel had in mind all along.

(And of course, because her eyes were dim, that wicked nasty old witch never noticed that Wolfdog was getting fatter and fatter every day, and was becoming the best of friends with Hansel and Gretel alike.)

But the day came, as it was bound to, when the witch had had quite enough of all this. "No more waiting!" she screeched. "I'll eat him as he is. Fetch the wood, Gretel. Light the oven. The oven needs to be hotter than hot, hotter than hellfire, you understand? I want him crispy on the outside, all crackling and crunch, and all tender on the inside. And whilst you're making the fire, I'll make some nice crusty bread to soak up the gravy."

As the old witch was bending over the kitchen table,

kneading the dough for the bread, she began humming a
cackling tune to herself, and the tune soon turned into a song.
But when Gretel heard the words of the song, it made
her tremble.

"*Two roast children, yummity, yummity yum. Which will be
spicier, girl or boy? Yummity, yummity yum. Which will be
nicier, girl or boy? We'll soon see, we'll soon see.*"

Gretel knew now that time was running out fast, for both of them. She had to do something, and quick. Back and forth she went, fetching the wood for the oven. Every time she climbed up onto the stool with more wood for the oven, the warty old witch would screech at her. "More wood! More wood! Faster! Faster! Dreaming, you're always dreaming, Gretel." But Gretel wasn't dreaming at all. She was thinking and thinking hard. She was waiting for her chance, waiting till the oven was stacked full of wood, waiting till the witch told her to light it.

"Now light it, Gretel, light it," croaked the warty old witch at last.

Gretel climbed up onto the stool again. "I've tried and I've tried, but I can't reach in far enough to light it," she said. "My legs are too short. My arms are too short."

"Just stick your head in!" cried the old witch. "You can reach if you stick your head in, you stupid girl."

"I've tried and I've tried," Gretel told her. "But I can't do it. My neck's too short."

By now the warty old witch had had quite enough of all this. She came hobbling across the kitchen, grumbling all the way. "Good for nothing," she said. "All children are the same, good for nothing, except eating." And with that she shoved Gretel aside off her stool and climbed up in her place. "Stupid girl. Stupid girl," she grumbled on. "This is how you do it. First you get up on the stool, like this. You put your arms in, like this. Then your head goes in, like this."

By now she was as high on her tippy toes as it was possible for her to be. "And now you light it, like this," she cried, her words echoing from deep inside the oven.

Gretel saw the flames rising and the smoke billowing. It was the moment she'd been hoping for, the moment she'd been waiting for, the moment she'd been longing for. With one huge heave-ho, she pushed that nasty, warty old witch into the oven, slammed the door shut, and bolted it fast. How the fire roared! How the old witch screeched and yowled! But Gretel wasn't there to hear it. She was already outside and setting Hansel free from his cage.

Then away they ran as fast as they could go, their friend Wolfdog bounding along beside them, his tail wagging wildly. He seemed as anxious to get away as they were.

All three of them stopped at the edge of the forest and looked back one last time at the old witch's cottage. And even as they watched they saw it all go up in a gigantic puff of smoke. When the smoke finally cleared the cottage was simply no longer there, and the warty old witch was gone with it. She had been burnt to cinders inside the oven, and the dreadful power of her wicked spells had died along with her (though the children did not yet know that).

But happy as Hansel was to be free at last, something was still worrying him deeply as they made their way, hand in hand, through the forest. "The old witch may be dead and gone, Gretel," he said. "But we still don't know our way home, do we?"

But at that moment Gretel was looking up.

"Look!" she cried. "Listen!" Above them like an arrow in the sky, flew a huge flock of geese. "They're pointing our way home, I know they are," she said. Everywhere they looked now there were birds, and they were singing, singing their hearts out. The whole forest had suddenly come alive again. All the trees were green again with leaves. Woodpeckers knocked in hollow trees, deer flitted through sunlit forest glades, wild boar grunted contentedly as they rooted about in the undergrowth. Wolves were there too slinking towards them through the trees, and when Wolfdog ran off to join them, every one of them howled with happiness to see him. Hansel and Gretel were not afraid, not one bit. As they looked about them they understood that all the wild things in the forest, from rabbits to robins, from otters and owls, and the wolves too, were protecting them and guiding them home. Every one of these creatures knew that the witch's curse was broken forever, and that they had Hansel and Gretel to thank for it. When Hansel and Gretel sang as they made their way through the forest that morning, it was not out of fear any more, but out of sheer joy. They were going home.

When at last they came out of the forest and saw their little cottage, they decided they would give their father a surprise. They tiptoed towards the door and threw it open.

"Here we are!" they cried. But there was no one there. They ran outside, and found him sitting on the river bank, still as stone. But he wasn't stone, and he wasn't alone either. Beside him was the lovely Lisette, her arm around him, no longer a willow tree, but herself again, his wife again, their mother again. There never was such a hugging as happened there then, by the bank of the rushing river.

With the warty old witch now dead and gone, and all her evil with her, the river teemed with fish again, the flowers bloomed, the bees and the butterflies flew again, and the trees and bushes filled with berries and nuts. The vegetables grew fat and sweet in the ground. The curse of the great hunger had been lifted, and all was right with the world and well again with the countryside, and the people of the forest were healthy and happy once more.

As for Hansel and Gretel, they told their tale again and again to everyone and anyone, because they loved telling it, and because everyone wanted to hear it. Then everyone and anyone told their children, and those children told their own children; which is why, all these long years later, I've been able to tell you the story of how Hansel and Gretel got rid of the warty old witch, and how the whole family really did live happily ever after.

The End

Michael Morpurgo

is the former Children's Laureate and has written over one hundred books. He is the winner of many awards, including the Red House Children's Book Award for his novel *Private Peaceful*. His books for Walker include *I Believe in Unicorns*, *Beowulf* and *Singing for Mrs Pettigrew*. He lives in Devon with his wife, Clare, with whom he runs the charity Farms for City Children.

Emma Chichester Clark

won the Mother Goose Award for *Listen to This*, and has been shortlisted for the Kate Greenaway Medal and the Kurt Maschler Award. She has created many acclaimed picture books for children, including the *Blue Kangaroo* stories and collections of fairy tales. Her books for Walker include *Not Last Night But the Night Before* and *Goldilocks and the Three Bears*. Emma lives in London.